HUSH, LITTLE BABY

HUSH, LITTLE BABY

Illustrated by

SHARI HALPERN

NORTH-SOUTH BOOKS

New York · London

Hush, little baby,
don't say a word,
Mama's going to buy you...

A MOCKINGBIRD.

And if that mockingbird
won't sing,
Mama's going to buy you...

A DIAMOND RING.

And if that diamond ring
turns brass,
Mama's going to buy you…

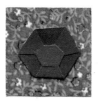

A LOOKING-GLASS.

And if that looking-glass
gets broke,
Mama's going to buy you...

A BILLY GOAT.

And if that billy goat
won't pull,
Mama's going to buy you...

A CART AND BULL.

And if that cart and bull
turn over,
Mama's going to buy you...

A DOG NAMED ROVER.

And if that dog named Rover
won't bark,
Mama's going to buy you...

A HORSE AND CART.

And if that horse and cart
fall down,

YOU'LL STILL BE
THE SWEETEST
LITTLE BABY
IN TOWN!

HUSH, LITTLE BABY

Gently

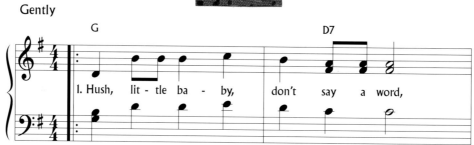

1. Hush, lit - tle ba - by, don't say a word,

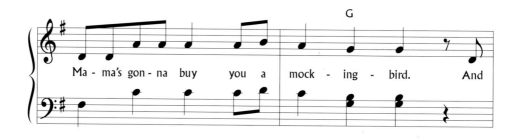

Ma - ma's gon - na buy you a mock - ing - bird. And

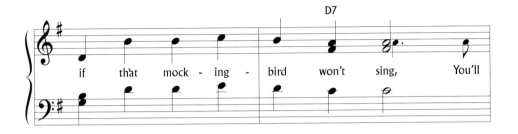

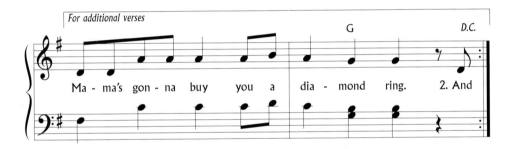

For the warm memories I have of
my mother, Jaclyn, who sang to me. —S.H.

Illustrations copyright © 1997 by Shari Halpern
All rights reserved. No part of this book may be reproduced
or utilized in any form or by any means, electronic or mechanical,
including photocopying, recording, or any information storage
and retrieval system, without permission in writing from the publisher.

Published in the United States by North-South Books Inc., New York.
Published simultaneously in Great Britain, Canada, Australia, and
New Zealand in 1997 by North-South Books, an imprint of
Nord-Süd Verlag AG, Gossau Zürich, Switzerland.

Library of Congress Cataloging-in-Publication Data is available.
A CIP catalogue record for this book is available from The British Library.

The artwork consists of collages made with several different types of paper painted
with acrylics and watercolors, and color photocopies of pieces of fabric.
Designed by Marc Cheshire

ISBN 1-55858-807-8 (trade binding)
1 3 5 7 9 TB 10 8 6 4 2
ISBN 1-55858-808-6 (library binding)
1 3 5 7 9 LB 10 8 6 4 2
Printed in Belgium

For more information about our books, and the authors and artists
who create them, visit our web site: http://www.northsouth.com